The Beautiful Kingdom

TROLL VALLEY

POISON FRUIT MARKET

KITTENS

⚠ PERIL

3 PIG CONSTRUCTION

Ⓞnce
upon a time
a beautiful Kingdom
stood high on a hill.
It had its share of danger,
but as long as you watched where you stepped,
and didn't go where you shouldn't,
it was a wonderfully happy place.

Until now . . .

. . . because the King had received warning of an Ogre, who was causing **mayhem**:

flattening trees, stamping on houses,

and **terrifying** everyone!

WARNING

King Hugo ordered his knights to capture the Ogre.

And he warned his three precious granddaughters,
Princess Thea, Princess Leaf and Princess Juno, to . . .

stay in their tower!
(And absolutely **not**,
on **any** account,
to
mess
with
the Ogre!)

"Mess with him?"
snorted Juno,
"He'd better not
mess with
us!"

"Besides," grinned Thea,
folding up the patchwork quilts
they were meant to be making,
"why should the knights have all the fun?"
"Come on," said Leaf, eyeing up the quilts. "I've got a plan!"

And soon the
three Princesses
were ready . . .

...to fly!

As they reached the forest, Sir Sniffle-Nose dashed
towards them, white-faced . . .
"You can't go this way!" he shouted. "The trees are alive!"
"Of course they're alive, Sir Sniffle-Nose!" replied Thea.
"It's an **enchanted forest!**"

unicorn petting zoo

Alive & pretty ticked-off
Enchanted Forest

It **was** enchanted
and **angry!**
Twisted, groaning trees
towered over terrified knights,
trussing them up and **snapping** their swords.

But the Princesses
sprang into the forest,

leaping,
twisting,

and whirling
through it.

"Watch out!"
gasped Leaf.

"Thank goodness for
our dance lessons!"
laughed Thea.

"And our hair,"
chuckled Juno,
"looks . . . fabulous!"

As they skipped away, Sir Clatter-Bottom and Sir Hairy-Toe
dashed by, shrieking . . .

"Spiders?" said Juno.
    "We're not
        scared of . . ."

"SPIDERS!"

yelped Thea and Leaf.

They had skipped into a webbed pit, squirming with
thousands of spiders that hissed and scuttled towards them.
"Um . . ." whimpered Leaf. "They're really . . . big spiders!"

"Don't worry, Leaf!"
called Juno,
grabbing a fallen branch.
She swiped at the spiders . . .

It **didn't** work!

"Juno, your mirror,"
Leaf whimpered.
"Dazzle them!"

It **still**
didn't work!

Then Thea had a brilliant idea.
She began to sing a beautiful, haunting tune.
And the spiders stopped,
and swayed, and fell . . .
fast asleep!

The Princesses
tiptoed through.

But beyond the pit . . .

CRASH!

SMASH!

"The Ogre!" gasped Thea.

He was on the other side
of a deep ravine and
the bridge was broken!
This was going to be tricky.

But Leaf wasn't worried,
"Tights off, girls!"

In a flash she'd made a long rope.

She tied her tiara to the end, and

with a

WHOOSH...

. . . they had a new bridge.

EASY!

Slowly,
carefully,
over they
went to the
other side,
where they
found . . .

CHAOS!

And the Ogre thundering off towards the next village.
"Quick!" shouted Thea. "We must stop him!"

The villagers, who'd been gaping at the Princesses, cried,

"Take our horses!"

"And this, please," called Leaf, coiling up a washing line.

The Princesses were off!
Faster and faster they galloped,
getting closer and closer to the Ogre.

Leaf hurled one end of
the washing line to Juno.

And before the Ogre knew it,
      they'd swept around him.

Again!

And again!

AND AGAIN!

"In the name of King Hugo," cried Thea, "you're under arrest!"

"Who said that?" groaned the Ogre.

"We
    did!"

"No . . ." The Ogre peered around. "Can't see you!"

"Well, you're still under arrest!" said Thea.

"Why?"

"Because," said Juno, "you've been causing mayhem: stamping and squashing the Kingdom!"

"Have I?"

"YES!"

"Oh dear!" moaned the Ogre,
"I hadn't realised. You see . . .
I've lost my glasses . . .
I can't see a thing!"

That explained everything!
The Ogre felt **terrible**.
"Come on!" sighed the Princesses.
"We'll help you find them."

And so, with the Princesses
sitting on the Ogre's shoulders
they searched . . .

HERE

THERE

and EVERY WHERE.

Until they found his glasses,
exactly where he'd last had them.

Back at the palace King Hugo
gathered everyone together.
"We're here to recognize great bravery . . ."

"Why, thank you!" Sir Clatter-Bottom bowed.
"It was nothing!" murmured
Sir Sniffle-Nose.

King Hugo gave them an odd look,
"As I was saying . . ."

"Golly!"
the Ogre stared
across the room.
"You're Princesses!"

"Oh, I
give
up!"
groaned the King,
and presented
medals to his
laughing
granddaughters.

"My dear girls," said King Hugo over dinner, "the next time there's a **terrifying** creature on the loose you won't go **messing** with it . . . will you?"

"Well . . ." said Juno.

"No, stop!" the King stuck his fingers in his ears. "I don't want to know!"

The End